SUPER
SPECIAL
#1

THE
WORLD SERIES
CURSE

Also by David A. Kelly

THE BALLPARK MYSTERIES

THE MVP SERIES

●●●

Babe Ruth and the Baseball Curse

SUPER
SPECIAL
#1

THE
WORLD SERIES
CURSE

by David A. Kelly

illustrated by Mark Meyers

A STEPPING STONE BOOK™
Random House 🏠 New York

*To all the independent bookstores (such as Newtonville Books
in my hometown) that help connect readers with great books.*
—D.A.K.

*To David A. Kelly, thanks for creating such a wonderful series of
mysteries with characters that are so fun to read about and to draw!*
—M.M.

*"Baseball was, is and always will be to me
the best game in the world." —Babe Ruth*

Text copyright © 2016 by David A. Kelly
Cover art and interior illustrations copyright © 2016 by Mark Meyers

All rights reserved. Published in the United States by Random House Children's Books, a division of Penguin Random House LLC, New York.

Random House and the colophon are registered trademarks and A Stepping Stone Book and the colophon are trademarks of Penguin Random House LLC. Ballpark Mysteries® is a registered trademark of Upside Research, Inc.

Visit us on the Web!
SteppingStonesBooks.com
randomhousekids.com

Educators and librarians, for a variety of teaching tools, visit us at RHTeachersLibrarians.com

Library of Congress Cataloging-in-Publication Data
Names: Kelly, David A. (David Andrew). | Meyers, Mark, illustrator.
Title: Ballpark mysteries super special. The World Series curse / by David A. Kelly ; illustrated by Mark Meyers.
Description: New York : Random House Books for Young Readers, [2016] | Series: Ballpark mysteries | "A Stepping Stone Book." | Summary: Mike and Kate must solve a mystery during a World Series between the Cubs and the Red Sox when someone starts ruining equipment, getting players in trouble, and even stirring up an old baseball curse.
Identifiers: LCCN 2015038986 | ISBN 978-0-385-37884-0 (paperback) |
ISBN 978-0-385-37885-7 (hardcover library binding) | ISBN 978-0-385-37886-4 (ebook)
Subjects: | CYAC: Baseball—Fiction. | Blessing and cursing—Fiction. | Chicago Cubs (Baseball team)—Fiction. | Boston Red Sox (Baseball team)—Fiction. | Mystery and detective stories. | BISAC: JUVENILE FICTION / Sports & Recreation / Baseball & Softball. | JUVENILE FICTION / Mysteries & Detective Stories. | JUVENILE FICTION / People & Places / United States / General.
Classification: LCC PZ7.K2936 Bal 2016 | DDC [Fic]—dc23

Printed in the United States of America
10

This book has been officially leveled by using the F&P Text Level Gradient™ Leveling System.

Random House Children's Books supports the First Amendment and celebrates the right to read.

Contents

A Goat Goes By

"Quick, take a picture of me in the Ted Williams seat before other fans get here!" Mike Walsh said to his cousin Kate Hopkins.

Mike and Kate were at Boston's Fenway Park for the fifth game of the World Series. The Red Sox were playing the Chicago Cubs, and the Cubs were ahead three games to one. Boston needed to win that night's game or their season would be over.

Mike dropped down into one of the seats in Fenway Park's bleacher section. The seats all

around them were green. But the one Mike sat in was bright red.

Mike pulled out an old-fashioned straw hat and slipped it on. Then he balanced a baseball on its brim and looked at Kate. Mike made funny faces as Kate snapped pictures and giggled.

"That's perfect!" Kate said. "It looks just like the ball is hitting you in the head!"

"That's the idea," he said. He popped up from the red seat. "This is where Boston's great hitter Ted Williams hit the longest home run at Fenway. It went through a fan's hat!" Mike swiped through the pictures on Kate's phone. "These are cool. I can post them on the website with the story I wrote about Ted Williams."

Mike and Kate loved baseball and visiting baseball stadiums. Mike even ran a website for kids about baseball.

Mike took a few pictures of the red seat in a sea of green seats. It was still two hours before game time, so the stadium was empty. "That is where the fan was sitting when it happened," he said. "The Red Sox made this seat red in celebration of that Ted Williams' hit."

When Mike finished taking pictures, he and Kate headed back into the hallways of Fenway Park to meet up with Kate's mom. She was a sports reporter. She had brought Mike and Kate with her to Fenway Park so they could watch the World Series while she worked in the pressroom. It was a dream come true for them!

"Kate! Mike!" said a voice.

"Hola," said another.

Mike and Kate turned around. It was Louie Lopez from the Chicago Cubs and Big D from the Boston Red Sox! They were just down the

hallway with bats in their hands. Big D and Louie jogged over to the kids.

Big D reached Mike and Kate first. "Hi, guys! Good to see you again," he said. "My two favorite detectives." Big D wore a big smile, like he always did. He was one of Boston's most popular players.

He was just about to give them a fist bump, when Louie reached out and did it first. Louie was the star center fielder for the Chicago Cubs.

"Hey! You know Mike and Kate, too?" Big D asked.

Louie nodded. *"Sí,"* he said. *"Mis amigos.* Mike and Kate are my friends. They helped us find out who was damaging the ivy at Wrigley Field!"

"Muy complicado," said Kate. "That was a tough mystery!" Kate was teaching herself Spanish. Her father was a scout for the Los Angeles Dodgers and worked with lots of players from other countries who spoke Spanish.

"Mike and Kate are great at solving mysteries," Big D said. "They helped me find my stolen bat the last time they were at Fenway."

"That's why I was hoping I'd run into them,"

Louie said. He looked at Mike and Kate. "I need your help. Someone's out to ruin the Cubs' chance to win the World Series!"

"Ha!" Big D said. "The only person who's going to mess up the Cubs' chance to win the World Series is me!" He pretended to give Louie a punch, and they play-wrestled for a minute. When they were done, they stood up and caught their breath.

"We can settle this tonight," Big D said, "on the field."

Louie lowered his head. "We can try," he said. "But someone *is* out to get us. Last night someone told the umpires that our pitchers were cheating by messing with the baseballs. The umpires found a bag with sandpaper and grease near our clubhouse. But I know that our pitchers weren't cheating."

"As long as your pitchers weren't cheating,

it shouldn't matter," Big D said. He shrugged. "Maybe it was a Red Sox fan. They like to try to rattle the other teams. Anyway, don't worry about it. We'll each have another chance to win tonight!"

Louie flexed his muscles. "I know," he said. "That's why I was just heading for the batting cage."

Before Big D could respond, they all heard a strange noise from behind them. There was

a clattering of hooves on the concrete floor.
It sounded like a horse galloping!

"Help me!" someone called out. "Catch him
before it's too late!"

Everyone wheeled around. They spotted a
woman in a yellow T-shirt. The shirt had a big
picture of a billy goat on its front. And there, just
a few feet away from her, was a billy goat with
big curled horns and a flowing white beard.

And it was charging right at them!

The Curse

The goat blew past them. Big D and Louie Lopez took off running to catch it, but Kate zoomed ahead of them. The goat skittered around a corner and started down a long brick hallway under the Fenway Park stands. It was headed for an open doorway and the sunshine outside.

Just as the goat was about to bound through the door, Kate snagged the length of cord that was dragging behind it and held tight. She slowed down and planted her heels.

Her sneakers slid for a moment on the concrete, and then the rope drew tight. The goat struggled to reach the door, but suddenly it stopped tugging. Louie, Big D, and Mike pulled up next to Kate. By this time, the goat had found an old bag of popcorn to nibble on.

"Thank you!" said the woman in the yellow shirt. She started scratching the goat's ears and gave it a big kiss. It nuzzled her back.

"What's a goat doing at Fenway Park?" Kate asked. She scratched the top of the goat's head gently.

"You've never heard of the Billy Goat Curse?" Louie asked. "It's followed us to Fenway. The guys on the Cubs think we might lose the World Series because of it!"

Mike and Kate shook their heads.

"I've heard about the Curse of the Bambino," Mike said. "That's when the Red Sox were cursed because they sold Babe Ruth to the Yankees."

"That's a different one," Louie said. "Ms. Sanders can tell you about the Billy Goat Curse. She's the owner of the Billy Goat Diner in Chicago."

The woman in the yellow shirt stood up. She shook hands with Mike and Kate. "I'm Sandra Sanders," she said. "A long time ago, the Cubs kicked my grandfather out of Wrigley Field because he brought his pet goat to the game. They said it smelled. My grandfather was angry that the Cubs made him leave, so he put a curse on the Cubs. He said the Cubs would never win another World Series because they weren't nice to his goat!"

Mike leaned over near the goat. He sniffed a few times. "Smells okay to me," he said. "But what's your goat doing here in Boston?"

"Well, my grandfather died a long time ago, so the Cubs are trying to lift the curse by being nice to me and my goat, Billy," Ms. Sanders said. "They've asked us to come to all the Cubs games this year. They hope that Billy will help break the curse, so the Cubs will win the World Series!"

Mike looked at Big D. "But aren't the Red Sox worried they'll lose if the Cubs break the curse?" he asked.

Big D waved his hand and laughed. "We don't care about a goat," he said. "Louie and his Cubs could bring a whole farm with them if they wanted. I don't think it's going to help them win the series this year."

"Well, we need all the good luck we can get," Louie said. He reached over to pet the goat.

Ms. Sanders handed Mike and Kate a business card for the goat. It read:

LET THE BILLY GOAT IN
AND LET THE CURSE GO!
THIS YEAR OR NEXT, IT'S THE CUBS!

The back of the card listed all the billy goat stuff Ms. Sanders sold, including Billy Goat Club memberships. It also gave the goat's website, where fans could send comments or ask for funny advice from the goat.

"Fans sure love the goat, even if they don't like the curse," Ms. Sanders said. "Billy and I keep really busy selling Billy Goat Curse hats, T-shirts, and more. If we're lucky, someday the curse will be broken. But hopefully not before Billy retires!" Ms. Sanders gave a short laugh that was interrupted by a man running down the hallway.

He was an older man in a blue dress shirt and a polka-dot bow tie. The man stopped right in front of the goat.

15

"Red, what happened?" Ms. Sanders asked the man. "You were supposed to be watching Billy while I was at lunch!"

Red brushed his hair back. "I was," he said. "I checked on Billy a few minutes ago, and he was tied up just where you left him. There was a man in a blue jacket talking on a phone near him, but everything was okay until I came back just now. Billy must have chewed through the rope."

"Well, Kate here caught him, so we're all set," Ms. Sanders said.

Louie slapped Red on the back. "Hi, Red! Good to see you," he said. "Mike and Kate, this is my good friend Red Remy. He's one of the most famous sports reporters in Chicago. Unfortunately, he's a big fan of Chicago's *other* major-league team, the Chicago White Sox. But at least he's not a fan of the Boston Red Sox!"

Red blushed and straightened his bow tie. He dropped his black messenger bag to the ground. "Well, the White Sox are my favorite team. But if they don't make the World Series, I guess the Cubs are the next best thing," he said. "But I hope next year it will be the White Sox!"

While they were talking, Mike examined the goat's rope. "Hey, this rope has a nice clean end. Someone must have untied him or cut the rope," he said.

Red laughed lightly. "Hmmm, it could have been that man in the blue jacket. I didn't think anything of it at the time, but he *was* near the goat."

Mike's eyes lit up. "What did he look like?" he asked. "Can you describe him?"

Red thought for a moment. "He was about my height. He had sandy brown hair. He was wearing tan pants and a blue jacket," he said. "And something about him looked a little shifty."

Kate leaned in to look at the rope while Red was answering Mike. Then she noticed the collar around the goat's neck. There was a luggage tag attached to it. Inside was a gray piece of paper with writing on it. The words were printed in block letters in thin blue ink.

"Um, Louie," she said. "I think this is for you." She pulled the luggage tag off the goat.

"Why, what does it say?" Louie asked.

Kate read the note.

THE BILLY GOAT CURSE STRIKES AGAIN!

Your Good Luck Goat Has Left the Building.
The Cubs Will Lose the World Series!

A Double-Crossing Goat

Louie's shoulders sank. "See? I told you!" he said. "Someone's out to get us!"

Kate tried to give him the tag, but he waved her off. "No, it's bad luck," he said. "I don't want it."

Kate studied the note. It was torn along its top. And the writing was neat, with letters that were more square than round. When she was done, Kate stuffed the note and the tag in the back pocket of her purple shorts.

Louie nudged Red and pointed to Mike and

Kate. "These two solved a big mystery for us at Wrigley Field a little while ago," he said. "It would make a good story for you if they solved this mystery, too."

Red nodded. "Wow, that's great," he said. He picked up his black messenger bag and pulled out a pen and a stack of index cards. He wrote something on the top one and handed it to Kate. "Here's my contact info," he said. "Let me know if you come up with any ideas on who's causing trouble for the Cubs."

"Um, sure," Kate said. She looked at the piece of paper. It said: RED REMY, CHICAGO SPORTS NEWS NOW, followed by his phone number. She folded the note and slipped it into her pocket.

"Well, I've got to get Billy tied up again," Ms. Sanders said. She nodded at Mike and Kate. "Thanks for catching him. Stop by tonight during the game and I'll take a picture of you two with Billy!"

Mike's and Kate's faces broke into wide grins. "Great!" Mike said.

The group split up. Louie and Big D went to their batting cages to practice. Ms. Sanders left to tie up her goat. Red Remy went back to working on a story.

When everyone had gone, Mike and Kate headed for their seats. The gates to Fenway had just opened, and fans were pouring in. The seats at the top of Fenway Park's giant left field wall, known as the Green Monster, were filling with people waiting for batting practice. Groups of families with Red Sox hats, T-shirts, and even Red Sox shoes streamed past Mike and Kate.

Kate's mom was waiting for them at their seats, near first base.

"Amazing view, Mrs. Hopkins!" Mike called out when he spotted Kate's mom. Their seats were a few rows back from the infield, with a great view of the Green Monster and the Boston skyline.

"I thought so," Mrs. Hopkins said.

Kate's mom had bought some hot dogs for dinner. The three of them sat in their seats and ate as one Red Sox batter after another took batting practice. The crowd stood up and cheered when Big D hit two balls over the Green Monster seats and out of the park!

Red Sox fans in red jerseys continued to

fill in the seats as batting practice finished. The setting autumn sun gave a golden glow to the green seats. As the air grew a touch colder and the sky got darker, the huge neon Citgo sign outside the park lit up in bright neon red and blue. It was a perfect fall night for baseball.

Kate pointed to Fenway's left field wall. "I think I just got my costume idea for our Halloween party!" she said.

Mike and Kate were going to have a big Halloween party that weekend, after the World Series was over. They had invited all their friends from school, but they were still trying to decide on their costumes.

Mike stared at the huge green wall. "You're going as a wall?" he asked. "Is that because you're *board*?"

"No! I can go as the Green Monster!" Kate

said. "I can use cardboard to make a big green wall that I can wear over my shoulders. I'll paint the scoreboard on it and everything. And then dye my hair green and paint my face green so I look scary, like a monster!"

Mike nodded. "That's a great idea," he said. His shoulders slumped. He rolled the baseball he always had slowly from one hand to the other. "Now *I* just have to think of a costume."

"Well, maybe since you're rooting for Chicago to win the World Series, we can think of something from Wrigley Field for you," Kate said. "Like the ivy!"

Mike and Kate had visited so many baseball parks that they didn't have favorite baseball teams. But for the World Series, they each decided to root for one team. Kate wanted Big D and the Red Sox to win. Mike wanted Louie and the Chicago Cubs to win.

Mike thought about it. "Hmmm ... I don't think I want to go as ivy, but maybe we can think of something else from Wrigley Field."

After the Red Sox and the Cubs finished batting practice, Mrs. Hopkins went to the pressroom to work. The stands were now packed. Out in the bleacher seats behind center field, a chant started. Soon it spread. Mike and Kate jumped up to join. They yelled and clapped in time to the chant. "LEEEET'S go, RED Sox!" Clap-clap. Clap-clap-clap! "LEEEET'S go, RED Sox!" Clap-clap. Clap-clap-clap!

A few of the Chicago Cubs fans shouted "Let's go, Cubs!" as loudly as they could, but it was no match for the home fans.

A short time later, Fenway Park's speakers crackled to life. "Welcome to Boston for the WOOOOOORLD SERIES!" the announcer boomed over the speakers. "Now it's time to plaaaaaaaaaaaay ball!"

Mike, Kate, and the rest of the fans stood up and cheered as the Red Sox took the field.

"I can't believe we're finally at a World Series game!" Kate yelled to Mike.

Mike smiled and pumped his fist. "I know!" he said. "This is great!"

But it didn't take long for the Chicago Cubs to quiet the Boston fans when they got up to bat. The first two Cubs players hit singles with no outs. Fenway Park fell silent as Loopy Lenfield, the Boston pitcher, faced the next Cubs batter.

His first two pitches were balls. But the Cubs batter swung at Loopy's third pitch. The ball sailed high into the outfield. Fans held their breath, and the runners on first and second waited.

But the crowd erupted into cheers as the fly ball dropped into Big D's glove. It was an out!

Luckily for Boston, Loopy quickly got the next two batters out. The top of the inning ended without the Cubs scoring. The bottom of the inning also went fast. Boston put one runner on base, but the next three batters got out to end the inning.

The fans cheered as the Boston players ran out onto the field again. They wanted Boston to win!

"I'm thirsty," Mike said as he stood up. "Let's go find a PowerPunch."

Kate followed him up the aisle and into the big hallway at the top of the row. Before they could buy the PowerPunch, Kate spotted something. She tugged on Mike's sleeve and pointed down the hall.

"There's Ms. Sanders and the goat!" Kate said. "Let's go get our picture taken."

Kate ran off down the hall. Mike followed her to a booth with Ms. Sanders and her goat. Behind them was a banner that read: Reverse the Billy Goat Curse! A group of Chicago Cubs fans were lined up waiting to get their pictures taken with the goat. One of them was trying on a T-shirt and hat.

When Mike and Kate finally made it to the front of the line, Ms. Sanders gave them a big smile and a high five. "Thank you for catching Billy," she said. "This one's on me. Just stand over there next to him."

Ms. Sanders positioned Mike on one side of Billy and Kate on the other. While she set up the camera, Mike leaned over in front of the goat.

"Hey, Billy," he said. "How'd you like a bite of this baseball?"

Mike held his baseball out. But Billy turned his head to the side. Mike moved the ball closer, but the goat turned his head some more.

"What's the matter? Don't you like baseball?" Mike asked.

Kate shook her head. "I think he likes baseball, just not *baseballs,*" she said.

Mike tried one last time. He waggled the ball in front of Billy's nose. "Is that true?" he asked. "You don't like baseballs?"

Just as Mike was about to give up, Billy lowered his head, leaned forward, and shot his nose up.

WHACK!

Billy's snout hit Mike's baseball from underneath. The ball flew out of Mike's hands and up into the air!

"Ha! That's what you get!" Kate laughed.

Mike's ball dropped into a plastic bin of Ms. Sanders's stuff. Mike ran after the ball. Ms. Sanders went over to check on the goat. Mike dug through the bin looking for his ball. After a minute, he ran back and stood with Kate.

Ms. Sanders snapped one picture after

another of Mike, Kate, and Billy. When she was done, she gave them a business card. "You can download your pictures here," she said. "I've set it up so they'll be free. Thanks again for catching Billy."

Mike and Kate bought PowerPunches on the way back to their seats. As they sipped their drinks, a big cheer rose from the field. Kate ran over to a doorway to see what was happening.

"It's the third inning and Big D's up!" she said. "It's still 0–0."

Mike looked over his shoulder at Ms. Sanders. They were far enough away so she couldn't hear them talk. He waved Kate back. "Come here," he said.

"But Big D's up!" Kate said. She looked at the field and then headed back to Mike.

Mike raised his eyebrows and stared at Kate. "This is even bigger!" he said. "You'll never believe what I found out!"

"What?" Kate asked.

"I can prove that Ms. Sanders doesn't want the Cubs to win like she says she does! She actually wants them to lose!" Mike said. "She's tricking everyone and causing all the trouble for Louie and the Cubs!"

A Close Call

Kate grabbed Mike's arm. "What do you mean?" she asked. "Ms. Sanders is a Cubs fan! Why would she want the Cubs to lose the World Series? Doesn't she want to break the Billy Goat Curse?"

Mike threw the baseball from one hand into the other. It made a smacking sound.

"Maybe not," he said. "If the Billy Goat Curse is broken, she won't be able to make all this money selling billy goat T-shirts and hats! Plus, maybe she's still mad at the Cubs for kicking her grandfather out of the game."

Kate looked back at Ms. Sanders and Billy. She *was* doing a lot of business.

"But that's just a guess," she said. "You don't have any proof it's her."

Mike smiled. "But I do have proof that she's planning on the Cubs losing! If you ask me, that's pretty strange for such a big Cubs fan."

He pulled out his phone. He tapped the screen a few times to show Kate some pictures. "I took this when I was looking for my ball in Ms. Sanders's stuff."

Kate's jaw dropped. Mike's picture showed a Billy Goat Curse T-shirt. But instead of reading, "The Cubs—World Series Winners," it said, "The Cubs—Better Luck Next Year!" On it was a picture of Billy wearing four bright red socks on his feet and a Red Sox hat on his head!

"Think about it. Ms. Sanders has been around

Fenway the whole time," Mike said. "She could have messed with the Cubs' baseballs. And she could have easily untied Billy today when no one was looking. And no one would suspect her since she *says* she wants the Cubs to win!"

"No one but you, Mike," Kate said. She tapped her foot. "It doesn't seem like she'd do it, but I guess she could have."

"We have to stop her before she does something else to the Cubs," Mike said.

Just then, a big roar went up from the crowd. Kate and Mike ran to the railing overlooking the field. The Red Sox had scored a run! There were runners on second and third, and the Red Sox were ahead 1–0 in the bottom of the third inning.

"Come on," Kate said. "Let's get back to the game. If the Red Sox end up winning tonight, they'll play again in Chicago. Then we can tell Louie and Red about the T-shirt we found in Ms. Sanders's bin. If she's messing up the Cubs, they'll be able to stop her."

Mike nodded. He and Kate raced back to their seats. By the time they got there, the Cubs were at bat again.

The next inning flew by. Both teams fought hard, but neither scored. Loopy Lenfield pitched really well for Boston. He didn't let the Cubs get any more hits until Louie got up in the fifth inning and hit a home run!

Mike popped out of his seat and cheered. "The Cubs have tied the game!" he yelled. "Go, Cubs!"

The score stayed tied for the next couple of innings. After the seventh-inning stretch, Kate's mother joined Mike and Kate in their seats.

As with the Cubs, the Boston bats had grown quiet. But in the bottom of the eighth, the fans cheered when Big D stepped up to the plate. The batter before him had hit a double. If Big D could get a hit, Boston might score!

Big D walked up to home plate. He spun his foot back and forth in the dirt and took a few practice swings. His arm muscles stood out in the bright lights.

The Cubs pitcher studied Big D and waited for the right sign from his catcher. He shook off two signs, and then nodded and stood up straight. A second later, the ball snapped out of his hand and flew toward home plate.

Big D turned on his heel and swung his bat around in the blink of an eye.

BAM!

The ball exploded off the bat. It shot straight over the shortstop's head and dropped between the outfielders. The Boston runner on second ran around third and headed for home! Big D rounded first and headed for second.

The Cubs left fielder grabbed the ball and hurled it toward the catcher. The Boston runner was almost home. He slid. The ball snapped into the catcher's glove. He brushed the leather against the arm of the Boston runner.

The umpire waited for a second as the dust died down. And then he swung his arms out to each side.

SAFE!

The Red Sox had scored on Big D's hit! They were ahead by one run now!

Unfortunately, the Red Sox couldn't make their luck go any further. The next Boston batter struck out and ended the inning. At least they were ahead.

When the Cubs got up in the ninth inning, they didn't have much luck, either. The first two batters got out. But then Louie walked up to the plate. Mike and the other Cubs fans stood up and yelled as Louie took a few practice swings. A chant started. "Looooou-IE! Looooou-IE! Looooou-IE!"

Louie dipped his batting helmet. He let the first ball fly by for a strike. But he unwound on the second pitch.

POW!

It was a huge fly ball! The ball flew toward the right field wall as the Boston outfielder raced back. He leapt up and stretched into the air. The top of the fielder's glove captured the ball.

"It's an out!" Kate called. She jumped up and down. "The Red Sox won! The Red Sox won!"

Mike slumped into his seat as the Boston fans celebrated. "Well, I guess at least that means the Cubs will get a chance to win the World Series in Chicago," he said.

"Yes, you're right, Mike," Mrs. Hopkins said. "But do you two know what else it means?"

Mike looked at Kate. They both shrugged.

Mrs. Hopkins smiled. "Well, it means I'll have to work for the rest of the World Series," she said. "So how would you like to come with me to Chicago for the last two games? We can get your homework from your teachers and take it with us."

A Muddy Mess

Clippity, clippity, clippity, clippity.

A strange sound echoed down the hallway under Wrigley Field.

Mike and Kate were crouched behind a big gray laundry cart. Mike peeked over the top of it. "What's that?" he asked.

Kate glanced around the side of the cart. The hallway was empty except for a security guard.

"Shh! Someone's coming!" she said. "Maybe it's Ms. Sanders and the goat!"

It was the afternoon of game six of the World Series. Mike and Kate had arrived early at Wrigley Field, the Chicago Cubs' ballpark. While Mrs. Hopkins was up in the pressroom, they were hiding in the hallway outside the Cubs' clubhouse to spy on Ms. Sanders.

Clippity, clippity, clippity, clippity.

"It's her! And the goat!" Mike whispered.

The sounds drew closer. Mike and Kate could hear voices. A moment later, a group of Chicago Cubs players came into view!

Mike rolled his eyes. "That wasn't the goat! It was only the players' cleats," he said once they had entered the clubhouse. "Maybe this wasn't a good idea."

Kate nodded. "Let's stay just a little longer," she said. "Then we can go visit Louie before the game."

They watched the hallway for the next fifteen minutes. A few players came and went, along with some trainers and a woman who looked like a reporter. They were about to give up and head into the clubhouse themselves when they heard another funny sound from the hallway.

Clippity-clop, clippity-clop, clippity-clop.

They crouched behind the cart and tilted

their heads to hear better. Ms. Sanders led Billy through the clubhouse door!

Kate jumped up. "Follow her!" she said.

Mike and Kate ran over, opened the door, and popped inside.

The room was humming with activity. Cubs players were getting ready for the game. Louie Lopez stood near his locker on the other side of the room. He was talking to Ms. Sanders. When Louie spotted Mike and Kate, he waved to them.

The goat bleated and clopped around as Mike and Kate walked over.

"Hi, Mike and Kate!" Louie called out. "Just who I wanted to see!"

"What's up, Louie?" Mike asked.

Louie was rubbing his hands together. He kept shifting his weight from one foot to the other and looking around.

"It's great to be back in Chicago for these

last two games," he said. "But I'm worried that someone is still trying to make the Cubs lose. We need some good luck in the clubhouse."

Kate petted Billy's head. "So that's why Billy and Ms. Sanders are here," she said.

Louie nodded. "Yup," he said. "I had Ms. Sanders bring Billy down so all the players can rub his back on their way out to the field for good luck!"

Mike and Kate smiled and nodded.

"Sounds like a plan, Louie," Kate said. "Maybe it will bring the Cubs luck!"

Mike nudged Kate and looked at Ms. Sanders. "Yeah, *bad* luck!" he whispered.

Louie smiled. "How about I show you around?"

"Sure," Mike said. But then he noticed a clubhouse attendant sitting in the corner. He had a stack of new baseballs and a white tub filled with brown goop. The attendant opened the first box of balls.

"Is he using baseball rubbing mud?" Mike asked. "I've always wanted to see it."

"Yup," Louie said. "Most people don't know about baseball mud. It's called Lena Blackburne Rubbing Mud. It comes from a secret place in New Jersey. It makes the balls easier for the pitchers to grip and easier for the batters to see. We have to put it on eighty new baseballs each game!"

Mike, Kate, and Louie walked over to watch. Ms. Sanders and the goat followed. The clubhouse attendant dipped a few fingers in the tub and covered the new balls with a thin layer of brown mud. He had muddied up about five balls when he stopped and looked at his hands. He raised his eyebrows and lifted his fingers up to his face. Then he sniffed them.

"Pew!" he said. "Yuck! Something's wrong with the rubbing mud!"

The attendant jumped up and ran to the sink. He rubbed his hands quickly under the water.

Louie looked closely at the tub of mud. He sniffed it, let out a gasp, and backed away. "Whoa!" he said. "There's *definitely* something wrong with that mud!"

Ms. Sanders walked over and picked up the tub of mud. She looked at the brown goop inside and took a sniff. Her nose wrinkled.

"That's not baseball rubbing mud," Ms. Sanders said. "That's goat poop!"

Cheating Cubs

"Goat poop?" Kate asked. "Someone put goat poop in the baseball rubbing mud?"

Ms. Sanders nodded. "That's what it smells like," she said.

Louie smacked his forehead. "Oh no," he said. "This is more bad luck for the Cubs. We're going to lose!"

Ms. Sanders patted Louie's back. "Come on, Louie," she said. "The Cubs still have a chance! My goat and I are here to help!"

That's when Mike got *mad*.

"No, you're not!" he said. "I think *you're* the one trying to get the Cubs in trouble. *You* put the goat poop in the rubbing mud! You want the Cubs to lose!"

Ms. Sanders took a step back. "Are you crazy?" she asked.

"Where else would the goat poop come from?" Kate asked. "There aren't a lot of other goats around the stadium."

"Someone stole it from me!" Ms. Sanders said. "I didn't say anything about it before because it was so weird."

"Someone stole your goat's poop?" asked Louie.

Ms. Sanders nodded. "When I'm at the ballpark with Billy, I always collect his droppings in a can. But when I went to tie Billy up after Kate captured him at Fenway, I noticed the tin was empty. I know it was half full that morning. I just thought maybe someone had emptied it into a garbage by mistake."

Louie straightened up. "See? She's not out to get us," he said.

Mike pulled out his phone. "I'm not sure about that," he said. "Think of all the money she'll lose if the Cubs win the World Series."

Ms. Sanders held up her hand. "Hold on," she said. "I *do* make money selling Billy Goat Curse stuff. But that doesn't mean I want the Cubs to lose!"

Mike swiped through the pictures on his phone. "Aha!" he said when he spotted the one he was looking for. Mike held the phone up.

"It sure looks like you're planning on the Red Sox winning this year," Mike said. "That's why you had this other T-shirt made."

Ms. Sanders looked at the phone and then burst out laughing.

"You think *I'm* the one causing trouble for the Cubs?" she said. "Just because you found that T-shirt?"

Mike and Kate nodded.

"Okay, well, explain this," Ms. Sanders said.

She reached into her bag and pulled out another T-shirt. This one was the same yellow color as the one Mike saw, but instead of Billy wearing red socks, it had a picture of him *eating* a pair of red socks. Underneath the picture it read: Time for a New Pair of Sox!

"I have to design and print T-shirts weeks in advance so they're ready right after the final game," Ms. Sanders said. "I need both winning and losing T-shirts because I don't know who will win! You only saw the losing one, but this is the winning one."

She handed the shirt with the goat chewing the red socks to Mike and Kate. They looked at it and gave it back.

"So you're not the one who untied the goat or called the umpires about the scuffed baseballs in Boston?" Kate asked.

Ms. Sanders laughed. "No," she said. "I want the Cubs to win as much as Louie does! I'd be happy to give Billy a year off. I would miss making some money, but I would pay anything to have the Cubs win the World Series."

"Well, I'll do everything I can so we win," Louie said. He looked at the smelly baseballs

and nodded to the attendant. "Let's get rid of those and get some fresh rubbing mud."

"I'm afraid you can't," said a voice from behind them. "That would be cheating!"

Everyone turned to look. It was one of the umpires! Right behind him was Red Remy, the reporter.

Louie wrinkled his nose. "But they stink," he said. "We can't use them in the game!"

"You're right," the umpire said. "I'll need to

keep them as evidence. We've had a report that the Cubs are trying to cheat."

Red stepped forward. "I got a phone call from a man with a deep voice telling me the Cubs were not preparing the baseballs right," he said. "But the man wouldn't tell me his name."

The umpire gathered up the smelly baseballs. He put them in a bag, along with the jar of rubbing mud. Then he closed the bag and stared at Louie. "There will be a full investigation," he said. "Once we find out who did this, they'll be punished. If it was someone on the Cubs, the team may be disciplined!"

A Bad Break

The umpire left the room. Louie shook his head. "More bad luck!" he said. "The Cubs are doomed!"

Red patted Louie on the shoulder. "Come on, Louie," he said. "I don't have to start work for a little bit. Let me grab your bat and we can go down to the batting cage to warm up. It'll get your mind off this trouble."

Louie nodded. "I'll see you two later," he said to Mike and Kate. Then he winked at Mike. "I hear you're rooting for the Cubs. Keep

your fingers crossed for me. I could use some
good luck."

Mike held up both his hands. He showed
Louie four sets of crossed fingers. "I've got you
covered, Louie," he said with a big smile.

Louie gave Mike a fist bump. "Thanks,
Mike," he said. He headed toward the door,
where Red was waiting with Louie's bat.

Mike and Kate followed them out into the hallway. Then they found their way to Wrigley Field's main walkway. All around, workers were busy getting the field and food stands ready for the sixth World Series game.

Mike pointed to the outfield wall. "Looks like the ivy has all grown back!" he said. Wrigley Field's outfield wall was covered in green ivy that had been planted to make the stadium seem like a park. It was so bushy that sometimes baseballs got lost in it! The last time Mike and Kate were at Wrigley, they helped figure out who had been cutting down chunks of the ivy.

Since it was still a while before game time, Mike and Kate spent the next hour exploring Wrigley Field. They started by taking pictures of themselves in front of Wrigley's giant hand-operated scoreboard.

Mike scrambled underneath the scoreboard and looked at the metal ladder that disappeared into the bottom of it. During their last trip to Wrigley, Mike and Kate had gotten to go inside the scoreboard.

Then Mike and Kate found their way to the upper level. They peered down over the side and watched fans stream into the stadium. Soon batting practice started. Mike and Kate watched as players hit one ball after another over Wrigley's left field wall. The balls fell into the street below, where fans scrambled to grab them.

When the game started, the Red Sox came out strong. The first batter, Eddie Storm, hit a single. The next batter nailed a double, knocking Eddie in for a run. The Red Sox were ahead by one!

It wasn't a good start for the Cubs. "Louie

and the team should put a uniform on the goat and get him on the field," Mike said to Kate. "Maybe that would bring some good luck."

"Well, Billy did hit your baseball pretty hard at Fenway," Kate said. "He might be able to knock one out of the park here!"

Mike laughed. He felt better a few innings later when Louie tied the game for the Cubs. But soon after, the Red Sox scored again.

"Argh!" Mike said. "The Cubs just can't catch a break."

"But maybe we can," Kate said. "Let's take a break and get some food!"

Mike jumped up. "That's a great idea," he said. He and Kate found their way to a food stand. They bought two giant hot dogs covered with mustard, onions, and super-bright neon green relish.

In the sixth inning, the Cubs fell further

behind when a Red Sox player hit a double and knocked in two runners. That put the Red Sox up by three runs.

When the Cubs got up to bat, they struck out one-two-three. The seventh inning wasn't any better. The Cubs got two runners on base, but then three outs in a row.

"Even I'm beginning to think the Cubs are cursed!" Mike said.

With two outs in the bottom of the eighth inning, the Cubs got two men on base, and Louie came up to bat. A home run would tie the game!

Louie took some practice swings. He dug his foot into the dirt and held the bat up high. He waved the tip of the bat in small circles above his shoulder.

Then the Red Sox pitcher made a mistake.

He threw a fastball down the middle. It was the perfect pitch for Louie! Louie unwound and swung the bat.

CRACK!

Louie's bat connected perfectly with the ball. But the ball bounced weakly down the third base line because the bat exploded into a dozen pieces!

Corked!

Louie sprinted for first base while his teammates advanced.

But seconds later, the home plate umpire held up his hands. Splinters of wood were everywhere, and something else had scattered across the field, too. The umpire picked up a few of the objects and called another umpire over. A moment later, they motioned to Louie and his manager.

The crowd booed. Louie and the Cubs manager had a meeting near home plate with the two umpires. They examined Louie's bat while another umpire tried to clean up the field.

Louie's manager began arguing with an umpire. The umpire pointed to the piece of bat in his hand.

"I'm not sure about this," the stadium's announcer said. "But it looks like the umpire thinks Louie might have used a corked bat!"

Instantly, a large "boo!" rose from the crowd. Cubs fans started a loud chant: "Lou-IE! Lou-IE! Lou-IE!"

"What's a corked bat?" Kate asked.

"It's when someone hollows out the center of a bat and fills it with cork or something else bouncy," Mike said. "It lets the player hit the ball faster and farther. But it's illegal."

Louie's manager continued to argue until the umpire took a couple of steps away. He swung his right shoulder back and threw his arm high over his head.

Louie was being ejected from the game!

"BOO!" yelled the Cubs fans. They pounded on the seats.

Kate shook her head. "It's not fair!" she said. "Louie wouldn't cheat!"

Mike nodded. "But it sure looks like there was something inside his bat," he said. "Maybe someone messed with Louie's bat just to get him thrown out!"

After Louie walked off the field, the game continued. But losing Louie took all the life out of the Cubs and their fans.

The crowd started to cheer a little in the ninth inning when the Cubs got up, but it was no use. The Cubs struck out one after another, one-two-three.

The game was over. The Cubs had lost. The World Series was tied. Whichever team won the next game would win the World Series!

As the crowd thinned out, Kate nudged Mike. "Look, Louie's by the dugout," she said. She hopped up and ran down the aisle. Mike followed.

Louie was walking back and forth on the field searching for something. He finally picked up the handle of a bat from the grass along the side of the field. When he saw Mike and Kate, he walked over slowly.

Louie didn't look directly at Mike or Kate. Instead, he shook his head and motioned at the umpires on the far side of the field.

"I can't believe it! They're suspending me for the last game!" Louie said. "I finally made it to the World Series, and I get kicked out now, when the Cubs need me!"

"That's horrible," Kate said. "What happened to your bat?"

Louie shrugged. "I don't know," he said.

"It was fine during batting practice. Someone messed with it! Look what they put inside!"

Louie tossed something to Kate. She caught it. It was a small, clear bouncy ball with sparkly gold stars inside it!

"A bouncy ball?" Kate asked. She handed the ball to Mike.

"Yup," said Louie. "Someone hollowed out the bat and filled it with these. They make the baseball go farther. When the bat broke, these fell out all over the field. The umpires took the rest of them for evidence, but they gave this one to me."

While Kate and Mike examined the ball, Louie unwrapped the tape from what was left of the handle of his bat.

"Just what I thought!" he said. "This isn't one of my bats! I always carve my initials in the handle, under the tape."

Mike and Kate looked at the bat. There weren't any initials. Someone had switched Louie's bat!

Louie turned to go. "I have to get back to my locker to pack up my things," he said. "Maybe I'll be sitting with you tomorrow watching the game."

Kate tried to return the bouncy ball to Louie, but he waved her off.

"I don't want that," he said. "It's bad luck. Maybe you two can turn it into some good luck for me before tomorrow!"

A Note from the Suspect

Kate pushed a piece of paper across the table to Mike. "It's all we have," she said. "There isn't much to go on."

Mike and Kate were in the pressroom at Wrigley Field. They had come early so Kate's mom could do some work. Mike and Kate were still trying to figure out who was after the Cubs.

Mike picked up the piece of paper. It was the note that Kate had found tied around Billy's neck back in Boston.

Kate tapped the note. "Check out the hand-writing," she said. "The *d*'s and *o*'s are boxy and square. All we have to do is find out who wrote this note and we'll know who's making the Cubs lose!"

Mike let out a sigh. "But that could be anyone!" he said.

Kate nodded. "But we know that it's someone who travels with the team or had access to both stadiums. And it's someone who can get into the clubhouse, because they swapped the mud."

"I wish we knew more about people who work for the Cubs," Mike said.

"Me too," Kate said. She twirled a strand of hair around her finger. "Hey, I know someone who does! Let's go ask Red Remy."

Mike's face broke into a wide smile. "Great idea," he said. "High five!"

They smacked a high five and then started walking down the long row of desks in the pressroom. Reporters' names were written in black marker at each desk so they would know where to sit. Mike and Kate walked along the back row of workstations looking for Red's name.

Red wasn't at his desk. He was standing on the next level with another reporter. They were talking and laughing.

"It's too bad it worked out this way," Red said. "This should have been the White Sox's World Series. Instead, we're stuck with the Cubs."

Mike grabbed Kate's arm and pulled her down under the rows of desks above Red. There was a small gap between the floor and the front of the desk. "Shh!" Mike whispered. Then he put his eye up to the small gap. Kate did the same thing.

It was easy to see and hear Red and the other reporter from their hidden spot under the desk!

"Back in Boston, it sure seemed like the Cubs were about to win the series," the other reporter said.

Red nodded. "I know," he said. "But it's good that Boston has come back. You know what I say. I've got two favorite teams: the White Sox, and whoever's beating the Cubs!"

The other reporter laughed. "Well, now that Louie Lopez is suspended, it looks like that will be the Red Sox tonight," he said.

Red giggled. "Just the way it should be," he said.

Mike's eyes widened as he looked at Kate.

"Follow me," she whispered, and tugged Mike's arm.

She crept out from under the desk and shot

back to the table across the room. Mike followed. When they got there, Kate pulled out the note from the goat again.

"Did you hear that?" Mike asked.

"Yes," Kate said. "And it made me think of something. Hang on." She stood up and fished around in her back pocket for something. A moment later, she pulled out another piece of paper and plopped it on the table next to the goat note. It was the index card that Red had written his contact information on for them back in Boston.

Kate lined up the notes and studied them. Her eyes widened. She tapped the goat note. "Do you see what I'm seeing?" she asked.

Mike stared at the notes and nodded. "Yup," he said. "They were written by the same person."

Mike was right. The *d*'s and *o*'s in both notes

were boxy and square. And the slope and spacing of all the letters and words matched. The handwriting was exactly the same!

"Red's the one who's been messing up the Cubs!" Kate said. "And now we know why."

"Because he's a White Sox fan!" Mike said. "He's trying to sabotage the Cubs so the Red Sox can win!"

"We've got to tell Louie," Kate said.

Mike was about to agree when something caught his eye. It was Red. He had a black bag slung over his shoulder, and he was opening the pressroom door.

"We don't have time," Mike said. "Red's taking off. We've got to follow him!"

A Called Shot

Kate and Mike followed Red as he wound his way through Wrigley Field. Red used his press pass to get by the security guards. Mike and Kate waited for a minute and then showed security the passes they'd gotten from Louie.

Red stopped just outside the Cubs' clubhouse. As he checked something inside his shoulder bag, Mike and Kate squeezed past some trash carts and hid behind a large pole. From their hiding point, they had a clear view of both Red and the door.

"We'd better document this," Kate whispered to Mike. She took out her phone and snapped a few pictures of Red. Then she turned on the video recorder just as Red reached into his bag and pulled out a small clear bottle of yellow liquid. He looked around to make sure no one was watching, and then took the top off and smelled it. His face scrunched up, and he stuck out his tongue. Red quickly capped the bottle.

"Are you getting this?" Mike whispered.

Kate nodded. She continued to record Red as he pulled two more bottles out of his bag. Red checked again to make sure that no one was around. Then he opened the clubhouse door a crack and threw all three bottles inside!

CRACK! CRACK! CRACK!

Mike and Kate could hear the bottles breaking open on the concrete floor. Red closed the door and moved around the corner. A strange smell wafted into the hallway.

Red called out to the security guard farther up the hallway.

"Help! Someone just threw something in the clubhouse!" Red said.

The security guard came running. But he stopped a few feet away. "Oh, man! What's that smell?" he asked. "It's like rotten eggs."

Red pointed down the hallway. "A man with a red hat just came and threw some stink bombs inside the Cubs' clubhouse!" he said. "I tried to stop him, but he got away."

"But *he's* the one who just threw the bottles in there!" Kate whispered.

"He's trying to blame someone else," Mike said. "He did the same thing when he let the goat loose! *He's* the troublemaker!"

"We've got to show this video to Louie,"

Kate said. "He's probably at the batting cage. We have to stop Red before he does anything else!"

Mike and Kate sneaked back past Red and the security guard. They ran through the hallways to the Cubs' batting cage. Louie was busy hitting pitches. Mike and Kate waved to catch his attention. Louie let the bat drop. He motioned for Mike and Kate to come over.

"You'll never believe what we just found!" Mike said. "Your friend Red is the one creating all the trouble for the Cubs! Check out this video!"

Kate pulled out her phone and showed Louie her video of Red. Then she showed him the handwritten notes, which matched.

"I can't believe it," Louie said. "But it sure seems like Red is doing something wrong. Let's go tell security."

A short time later, Mike and Kate were in the ballpark's security office. They showed the chief of security all their evidence. When they were done, the security woman radioed for someone to bring Red up. She asked Mike, Kate, and Louie to wait in the hallway.

A few minutes later, Red showed up with a security guard. After half an hour, the chief of security came out with Red. She stopped in front of Louie, Mike, and Kate. Red kept his head down. He had taken off his bow tie.

The chief of security held up Red's bag. "Louie, you'll never guess what we found in here," she said. The chief reached in and pulled out a bag filled with clear star-filled bouncy balls.

Mike pulled the bouncy ball Louie had given him out of his pocket and held it up next to the bag. "They're the same," he said. "Red must have corked the bat and switched them when you practiced!"

The chief of security held up a clear bottle. "And these are the stink bombs that Red used," she said. "He was hoping they'd clear out the clubhouse and upset the Cubs. He tried to blame it on the made-up criminal, but your video fixed that!"

"How could you?" Louie asked.

Red stared at the floor. "I'm sorry, Louie," he said. "I like you, but the White Sox are the only team that matters in Chicago. If they can't win the World Series, the Cubs shouldn't!"

Louie took a deep breath and pulled back his shoulders. There was fire in his eyes.

"Well, Red, I'm afraid it won't work," he said. "The World Series isn't over! And even if I can't play, I can still sit on the bench and cheer my team on. The Cubbies aren't done yet!"

A Tiebreaker

While they waited for the World Series to start, Kate leaned forward and scanned the Cubs' bench for Louie.

"Well, I still want Big D and the Red Sox to win," she said. "But it's such a shame that Louie can't play."

Mike nodded. "The Cubs could really use Louie tonight," he said. "This is it. One of these teams is going to win the World Series!"

Kate's mom leaned over. She had written her story early that night, so she was able to watch the game with Kate and Mike. "But at least you two stopped Red," she said. "Now each team will have a fair chance to win."

Kate twirled her long hair around the tip of her finger. "I guess," she said. "But it would be even fairer if Louie were playing. He didn't have anything to do with that corked bat."

The Wrigley Field loudspeakers boomed to life. Both teams stood in front of their dugouts for the national anthem. When it was done, the Red Sox ran off the field to get ready to bat. The Cubs were just about to take the field when the loudspeakers crackled.

"Hold on, everyone," the announcer said.

Mike and Kate looked at each other.

"The umpires have reviewed new information from yesterday's corked-bat incident," the announcer said. "There's going to be a change in the lineup."

A figure ran out from the dugout to the middle of the infield with his head down. It was a Cubs player. When he reached the pitcher's mound, the announcer's voice boomed throughout the ballpark.

"It's LOOOUIE LOPEZ!"

The Chicago fans screamed and yelled. Louie lifted both arms in victory and looked around the stadium at all the happy fans.

"Louie's suspension has been removed," the announcer said. "The umpires decided that Louie didn't have anything to do with the corked bat."

Almost everyone in Wrigley stood and clapped. Slowly, a chant spread across the stadium from the bleachers.

"Lou-IE! Lou-IE! Lou-IE!"

It grew louder and louder until Louie took off his hat and bowed to the crowd. Then he motioned for the rest of his team to take the field. The Cubs ran out to their positions.

The Chicago Cubs got off to a great start.

In the second inning, Louie hit a double for the Cubs. The next batter struck out, but the following Cubs batter hit a single. Louie ran like a tornado and slid into home just as the throw landed in the catcher's glove.

"*Safe!*" called the umpire.

The Cubs were up 1–0!

Big D came out swinging in the next inning. He was close to hitting a home run, but the Cubs outfielder jumped high into the air and caught Big D's ball. It turned the hit into an out.

The Cubs stayed ahead by one run until the eighth inning. The Cubs pitcher struck out the first two Red Sox batters. Then the third batter hit a blooper that fell in for a base hit. On the next two pitches, the Boston runner stole second base, and then third. He was close to home. Kate and other Boston fans at Wrigley were going wild! It was one of the best chances all night for Boston to tie it up.

And that's exactly what they did. When

the next Boston batter hit a long line drive for a double, the runner on third ran for home. The outfielder threw the ball in, but it wasn't even close.

Boston scored a run! The final World Series game was tied, 1–1.

The Cubs fans grew silent. The cool fall air seemed to grow chillier. A few Boston fans cheered, but all eyes were focused on the Cubs pitcher. He needed one more out to keep Boston from scoring the go-ahead run.

The pitcher ground the ball into his hip. The bat buzzed back and forth with practice swings. The Cubs pitcher waited for the right sign from his catcher and let the ball fly.

POW!

The bat connected with the ball and sent it sailing high into the dark sky.

Cubs outfielders ran to get under the ball.

The Red Sox runner raced toward home. And the batter ran for first base.

The ball arced up and then down. The runners rushed around the bases.

But before the first runner crossed home plate, the ball dropped neatly into the glove of the Cubs left fielder.

It was an out!

The Red Sox players took the field for the bottom of the eighth as the Cubs got ready to bat. But Chicago's luck didn't change. Instead of getting on base, the first two Cubs batters struck out. The crowd clapped loudly for the third batter. But he hit a high pop fly that the Red Sox catcher caught.

The eighth inning was over. The game was still tied, heading to the ninth!

The Red Sox needed to score to win the game. Their fans cheered when the first Red

Sox batter hit a single. But hope turned to despair when the second batter hit into a double play to give the Red Sox two outs. Even Big D couldn't save the day. He watched two strikes go by and then hit a line drive to first base for the third out.

As the Cubs ran off the field, their fans clapped and yelled. Now was their chance! If the Cubs scored a run, they'd win the game and the World Series!

But it wasn't going to be easy. As the Red Sox took the field, the pitcher warming up threw one strike after the other.

SMACK! SMACK! SMACK!

The balls popped into the catcher's glove like explosions from a cannon. The game wasn't over yet.

It looked like the first Cubs batter might win the game when he hit a long drive into right field. The fans cheered as he ran. But the right fielder grabbed it on a bounce and hurled it to second base.

It was close, but the Cubs player was out!

Louie was up next. The stadium filled with what sounded like choruses of fans shouting "Boo!" But they were actually calling "Lou!" as Louie walked to the plate.

Louie was focused only on the pitcher. When the ball came hurtling toward him, he swung and hit it with all his might.

The ball sailed down the third-base line. It slipped past the third baseman and into left field. Louie rounded first and headed to second.

He hit a double! The Cubs had a runner on base and only one out.

As the crowd cheered, Louie's teammate Dexter Russell walked up to the plate. He watched as the Red Sox pitcher threw two

balls. Dexter was waiting for the right pitch. The pitcher tightened up. He stared at Dexter and threw a high fastball.

Dexter liked it. He swung. The bat chopped down and hit the ball at just the right angle.

POP!

The ball launched off the bat and down the right field line. Louie raced around the bases.

The Red Sox right fielder tried to grab the ball
but booted it with his foot and sent the ball fly-
ing! Louie rounded third. The fans screamed
themselves hoarse.

The right fielder found the ball and rifled it
home.

Louie and the ball were both racing toward
the catcher. Louie dove for home plate. His

hands stretched out in front of him while he angled his body away from the catcher.

The throw from the outfield snapped into the catcher's glove. The catcher swung the glove down to meet Louie.

Dust flew. The umpire motioned with his arms. The play was over!

The crowd couldn't believe the call.

A Winning Series

SAFE!

Louie had scored! The Cubs had won the World Series!

Mike, Mrs. Hopkins, and even Kate jumped up and cheered. The Cubs players mobbed Louie at home plate.

The Red Sox players slumped off the field. This wasn't their year. Big D tipped his hat as he walked by the clump of celebrating Cubs players.

One of the batboys ran out and sprayed seltzer on the team. The jumbo TV screen in left field showed big close-ups of Louie and the other Cubs players having fun.

The fans went crazy when the commissioner of Major League Baseball presented the World Series trophy to the Cubs. After that, nobody seemed to want to leave. It took forever for the Cubs players to clear the field. And the fans stayed even longer. Mike and Kate continued to clap and yell for the Cubs.

More than an hour after the game was finished, fans finally started leaving. The infield was mostly empty, although a few reporters were still recording stories. Mike and Kate were getting ready to go when a Wrigley Field usher came up to them.

"Louie is waiting for you over there," the usher said, pointing to the far side of the Cubs' dugout. "He'd like to talk to you."

Kate and Mike high-fived. "Hang on, Mom," Kate said. "We can't leave yet! Mike and I will be back in a minute!"

She and Mike ran through the seats until they came to the edge of the Cubs' dugout. The only other fans left were streaming out of the exits.

"Mike and Kate!" called a voice. "Just who I wanted to see."

Louie stepped out of the shadow of the dugout. He gave Mike and Kate a fist bump. Big smiles spread across their faces.

"Thanks, Louie," Kate said.

"And they're just who *I* wanted to see!" said another voice. A player in a Boston Red

Sox uniform stepped out from behind Louie.

It was Big D!

Big D reached over and gave Mike and Kate two big hugs.

"Even though we lost the game, you two

were great again!" Big D said. "I *told* Louie that you'd figure out where his bad luck was coming from."

Mike gave Big D a funny look. "But aren't you sorry you lost the game?" he asked. "I would be."

Big D tilted his head back and let out a big belly laugh.

"I'm so happy just to be *in* the game, Mike," Big D said. "Plus, no one deserves to win more than Louie and the Chicago Cubs! It's been a long, long time!"

Louie gave Big D a high five.

"Thanks, brother," he said. "Tell you what. Let's meet back here next October for a rematch. I'd be happy to give you and the Red Sox another chance!"

"You got it!" Big D said. "I guess we're done

for this year. Maybe it's time to get ready for Halloween."

Mike's eyes grew wide. "My Halloween costume! I haven't thought of one yet," he said.

"Don't worry, we will," Kate said. She looked at Big D and Louie. "Mike and I are having a big Halloween party on Saturday. Now that you're done with the World Series, how'd you two like to come?"

Louie looked at Big D and shrugged. "I don't know, maybe," he said. "Sounds like a lot more fun than this series!"

Big D smiled. "I love parties," he said. "But we'll have to think about it. I haven't had time to figure out my costume for this year. But maybe I could go as an umpire. They're plenty scary!"

The kids laughed. Big D clapped Louie on the back, and they turned to go.

"Thanks for inviting us," Louie said. "And thanks even more for saving the World Series!"

Trick and Treat!

Ding-dong!

Kate's doorbell in Cooperstown, New York, was ringing. It was Saturday night, and she and Mike were hosting a Halloween party at her house near the National Baseball Hall of Fame. They had invited all their friends from school. Mike and Kate had picked a special theme. It was a World Series Halloween party! Everyone could come as anything they wanted to, like a ghost, a zombie, a ballerina,

a dog, or a TV star, as long as they had something baseball-related on them!

Kate opened the door. A rush of chilly fall air swirled inside. Outside was a surprising sight: a long, tall hot dog in a bun, with mustard, ketchup, bright green relish, and a Chicago Cubs World Series baseball hat!

"Trick or treat!" said a voice. "The Halloween hot dog is here!"

Kate giggled. "Mike, that's GREAT!" she said. "I knew you'd come up with something for your costume!"

Kate stepped aside and let Mike in. Mike's hot dog costume went from above his head down to his feet. He wore white sneakers and big white cartoon gloves.

"What do you think?" Mike asked.

"You look like the best hot dog ever, Mike!" Kate said. "Especially if you're a Chicago Cubs fan! How's my costume?"

Kate was dressed as the Green Monster. She had taken a big cardboard box and cut out a hole for her head on the top, and holes for her arms out the sides. But the front and back of it were painted dark green to match Fenway Park's giant left field wall. And she had painted her face green and wore a funny green wig.

"Second-best costume ever!" Mike said. "Sorry it's not as *hot* as mine! Get it? I'm a *hot* dog!"

Kate groaned. "Okay, okay," she said. "Quick, let's finish setting up!"

Mike and Kate had spent the past few days getting ready for the party. They cut out and colored huge figures and taped them to the walls of Kate's house. There were vampire umpires, zombie baseball players, and even ghost pitchers!

Mike and Kate helped Kate's mom put out snacks and set up some spooky games. Mike put on some haunted-house music.

"AHHHHHHHH!"

A scream filled Kate's house. Kate's mom dropped a bowl of potato chips and it flew all over the floor!

"Ha-ha! Got you!" Mike said.

Kate's mom shook her head. "No fair, Mike," she said. "You didn't tell me you were going to turn on the haunted-house music."

"Haunted-house music?" Kate asked. "I thought that was Red Remy's scream when he learned that he was going to have to give up his TV show and go to jail for messing up the Chicago Cubs."

Mike scratched his head and looked at the speaker. "It *did* sound a little like him, didn't it?" he asked.

Kate's mom bent over and started to sweep the potato chips into a pile. "Well, if it was him, I wish he'd help pick up all these chips," she said.

Mike and Kate laughed and walked over to help. Mike's music continued in the background with groans, creaking doors, and howls of wind. Another scream split the night just as they finished picking up the mess.

"Now *that* sounds like the Red Sox fans!" Mike said. He elbowed Kate. "Too bad the Cubs won it this year!"

Kate smiled. "I'm not worried," she said. "There's always next year!"

Before long, the house was crowded with all types of baseball ghosts, goblins, and scary creatures. The evening started off with a doughnut-eating contest. But instead of just eating doughnuts, the kids had to try to eat doughnuts hanging on strings from the ceiling without using their hands! Next up, they tried bobbing for apples in a big bucket of water and playing pin the broom on the witch. And Mike walked around with a covered bowl filled with peeled grapes and asked everyone to feel the eyeballs he had collected!

About halfway through the party, there was a loud knock on the door. Mike and Kate raced to open it.

The night was pitch-black, without a moon. Some leaves rustled along the side of Kate's house.

"I don't see anyone," Mike said. "Maybe it was a ghost!"

Kate peered into the darkness. "That's weird," she said.

Mike stepped back inside. Kate had started to shut the door when two figures bounded out of the bushes on either side of the front door!

"BOO!" they yelled.

Mike and Kate both jumped straight up!

Two large figures stood in front of them. One was dressed as a New York Yankee. The other was dressed as a St. Louis Cardinal. Both had big black umpire masks on.

"Who's that?" Kate asked.

The players howled with laughter and took their masks off.

It was Big D and Louie Lopez!

"We couldn't resist your Halloween party," Big D said.

"But what's with the crazy costumes?" Mike asked. "Did you switch teams?"

"No! The scariest things we could think of were our biggest rivals," Big D said. "But then we decided to add the umpire masks to make our costumes even scarier!"

Mike and Kate laughed. Then Big D threw his arm around Louie's shoulders and pointed to Mike and Kate.

"You two saved the World Series," Big D said. "Even if the Red Sox didn't win this year, at least the Cubs won fair and square."

Louie gave them a big smile. "Winning

the World Series was great," he said. "But spending time with friends like Mike and Kate is even better!"

Big D nodded. "That's a World Series win for me any day!" he said.

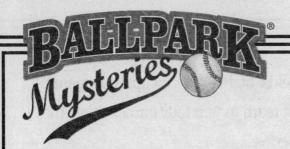

Dugout Notes

☆ SUPER SPECIAL ☆
The World Series Curse

The World Series. The World Series is baseball's big finish each year. It's a series of up to seven games played between the two best teams in baseball. One team is from the American League, and the other team is from the National League. The World Series is played in October and is split between the home fields of the two competing teams. The first team to win four games takes the World Series.

World Series winners. So far, the team with the most World Series wins is the New York Yankees. Through 2015, the Yankees had a total of twenty-seven World Series wins. The St. Louis Cardinals have the next most World Series wins, with eleven. Between 1920 and 1964, the Yankees played in twenty-nine World Series and won twenty of them. They even won it five times in a row, starting in 1949.

The Billy Goat Curse. Some people do really believe that the Billy Goat Curse is responsible for the Cubs' bad luck over the years. It started in game four of the 1945 World Series. William Sianis, the owner of the Billy Goat Tavern in Chicago, tried to bring good luck to the Cubs by taking his pet billy goat to the game. He even bought a ticket for the goat. But the ticket takers wouldn't let the goat in. The Cubs owner wouldn't let him in, either. He said the goat stank! Sianis stomped off with his goat and cursed the team. According to legend, he said, "The Cubs ain't going to win no more. The Cubs will never win a World Series so long as the goat is not allowed in Wrigley Field."

The Curse of the Bambino. The Red Sox had their own curse. After the Red Sox sold Babe Ruth to the New York Yankees in 1919, they started to lose important games. They also didn't win a World Series for many, many years (eighty-six, in fact). But the Yankees went on to win many World Series. Some people said the Red Sox were cursed because they had sold one of the best players of all time to their rivals. To learn more, read *Babe Ruth and the Baseball Curse.*

Lena Blackburne Rubbing Mud.
Baseball teams don't use new baseballs right out of the box. Instead, before each game, teams rub new baseballs in mud! The mud is called Lena Blackburne Rubbing Mud. It comes from a secret place in New Jersey. The mud takes the shiny gloss off the white leather and makes the balls easier for batters to see. To learn more, read *Miracle Mud: Lena Blackburne and the Secret Mud That Changed Baseball.*

First World Series. The first World Series was held in 1903. The Pittsburgh Pirates played the Boston Americans

(who later became the Boston Red Sox).
Boston won the series.

Getting there. Originally the team with
the best record in each league (National
and American) went to the World Series.
But since 1969 there have been playoffs (the
American League Championship Series
and the National League Championship
Series) to determine which two teams will
play in the World Series.

The American League is ahead.
Overall, the American League has won
more World Series than the National
League. As of 2015, the American League

has sixty-four wins, and the National League has forty-seven.

Trophy. The winner of the World Series gets the Commissioner's Trophy. It has a big round base with tall gold flags that ring the edges. The flags represent each of the major-league teams.

Earthquake. There was even an earthquake during the World Series. On October 17, 1989, the San Francisco Giants were playing the Oakland Athletics in San Francisco. It was just before the start of game three when an earthquake struck. The Loma Prieta earthquake was strong—it caused the stadium to move back and forth. The quake knocked out power and caused damage to the upper deck of Candlestick Park. The game had to be stopped and played ten days later.

Heading north. The World Series was played outside of the United States for the first time in 1992, when the Toronto

Blue Jays from Canada played the Atlanta Braves. That truly made it a *World* Series.

Home-field advantage. The World Series is up to seven games long. The first team to win four games wins the series. If the series goes to seven games, the teams play four games at one stadium and three at the other. That means one team gets to play an extra game at their home field, where the cheering fans may give the home team an advantage. The teams split up the games so that each team will have some home games at the start. The first two games are played on one team's field. Then the series moves to the other team's stadium for the next three games. If there isn't a winner, the games return to the first team's stadium for the last two games. The team (or league) that gets the home-field advantage is decided by the All-Star Game in July. For example, if the National League team wins the All-Star Game, the National League team in the World Series gets home-field advantage.

Get ready for more baseball adventure!

Did Babe Ruth curse the Boston Red Sox when he moved to the New York Yankees?

Available now!

New friends. New adventures. Find a new series . . . just for you!

BALLPARK *Mysteries*
FOR THE SPORTS FAN

DINO FILES
FOR THE ADVENTURER

Louise Trapeze
FOR THE SUPERSTAR

PIPER GREEN
FOR THE DREAMER

PUPPY PIRATES
FOR THE ANIMAL LOVER

adventures!
FOR THE EXPLORER

Illustrations (from left to right): © Mark Meyers; © Mike Boldt; © Brigette Barrager; © Qin Leng; © Russ Cox; © Wesley Lowe

RandomHouseKids.com